THE THANKFUL SMURF

by Peyo

Simon Spotlight

New York   London   Toronto   Sydney   New Delhi

SIMON SPOTLIGHT

An imprint of Simon & Schuster Children's Publishing Division

1230 Avenue of the Americas, New York, New York 10020

© Peyo - 2012 - Licensed through Lafig Belgium - www.smurf.com. All Rights Reserved.

Originally published in French in 2003 as *Un Schtroumpf pas comme les autres* written by Peyo.

English language translation copyright © 2012 by Peyo. All Rights Reserved.

All rights reserved, including the right of reproduction in whole or in part in any form.

SIMON SPOTLIGHT and colophon are registered trademarks of Simon & Schuster, Inc.

For information about special discounts for bulk purchases, please contact Simon & Schuster Special Sales at 1-866-506-1949 or business@simonandschuster.com.

Manufactured in the United States of America 0912 LAK

10 9 8 7 6 5 4 3

ISBN 978-1-4424-5292-3

Life was peaceful in Smurf Village, and the Smurfs went about their work in good spirits. Most of them never even thought of leaving the Land of the Smurfs.

All except one Smurf: He often had a sad, distant look on his face. He was so different from the other Smurfs!

When his friends invited him to play with them, he always said no, even though he looked bored. They called him the Wandering Smurf.

The Wandering Smurf had a secret. He was tired of everyday village life and dreamed of traveling to faraway places where everything would be new and different.

One day the Wandering Smurf decided he had had enough. He told Papa Smurf that he was leaving the village to travel around the world and that no one could stop him.

"Leave if you want to, but take this magic whistle," said Papa Smurf. "If you're ever in danger, blow on the whistle and it will transport you straight back to Smurf Village!"

The Smurfs were sad to see the Wandering Smurf go, but they wished him well on his journey.

The Wandering Smurf was happy as he walked into the woods, leaving Smurf Village behind him. He felt as free as a bird and could already picture himself climbing mountains and crossing oceans!

After a day of walking, the Wandering Smurf made himself a cozy bed on the forest floor. The forest was full of scary noises, and he shivered with fear. He thought about using his magic whistle, but he was too proud to go back to the village so soon. Exhausted, he finally fell asleep.

The next day it rained and rained and rained.

When the sun finally came out from behind the clouds, the Wandering Smurf began to feel better. He perched himself on a log and floated down the river.

The Smurf had no idea he was heading straight toward danger! Gargamel was just downriver, fishing with his nasty cat, Azrael.

The poor Smurf didn't even have time to realize what was happening when Gargamel scooped him up in his net! Soon the Wandering Smurf was tied up and locked in Gargamel's cottage.

"What's this?" asked Gargamel, as he picked up the magic whistle. He brought the little whistle to his lips and blew on it . . .

Gargamel was instantly transported to Smurf Village!
"I've finally found it!" Gargamel said. As soon as he recovered from his surprise, he threw himself into chasing after the Smurfs. Terrified, the little blue Smurfs scattered in all directions, hoping to escape.

Even Papa Smurf was in shock. "Gargamel is here?" he said. "Oh no!"

Papa Smurf quickly prepared a special potion. It was the Smurfs' only hope against Gargamel! A few minutes later Papa Smurf ran outside, holding a test tube filled with liquid.

"Over here, you big brute!" Papa Smurf yelled, as he ran toward Gargamel.

Gargamel grabbed Papa Smurf. "Aha! I've got you at last, you miserable little pest!" he cried, triumphantly.

But Papa Smurf threw the contents of the vial into the evil wizard's mouth. Soon Gargamel began to wobble. He was dizzy and confused.

Moments later a change came over Gargamel.

"My dear little Smurfs," whispered Gargamel, sitting on the ground. "Why are you running away from me? I don't want to hurt you!"

Papa Smurf's magic potion made Gargamel gentle and kind!

"How did you find us?" asked Papa Smurf.

"Well, now, I'm not sure," replied Gargamel. "I had just taken your friend's whistle and . . ."

"You captured the Wandering Smurf! What have you done with him?" demanded Papa Smurf.

"He's at my cottage, of course! Dear sweet Azrael is watching him."

"What?" cried Papa Smurf. "That nasty old cat will eat him for breakfast!"

"We have to rescue him!"
Gargamel said, running full speed
ahead. The Smurfs tried to keep up
with him.

Papa Smurf was right. Back at Gargamel's cottage Azrael was making the most of his master's absence and was chasing after the Smurf. The Wandering Smurf ran in every direction, trying to escape, but Azrael had him cornered and was ready to pounce.

At that exact moment the cottage door burst open.

"Stop, you horrible creature!" cried Gargamel, lunging toward the cat. "Don't hurt this poor little Smurf!"

Azrael didn't understand. His master was acting *very* strange.

The Smurfs arrived soon after and were relieved to find the Wandering Smurf, safe and sound. They were so busy with their joyful reunion that they didn't realize that Gargamel was changing. The effects of the magic potion were already starting to wear off.

Soon the wizard became as mean and cruel as always. He slammed the door, picked up his net, captured all the Smurfs, and locked them in a cupboard.

"This is terrible!" one Smurf whimpered. "This time he'll smurf us all!"

"What if we smurfed this?" another Smurf suggested, holding up the magic whistle. "Gargamel dropped it in the village!"

"Quick, everyone, hold hands!" whispered Papa Smurf. He blew on the magic whistle, and the Smurfs were all transported back home.

Back at his cottage Gargamel got a shock when he opened the cupboard door.

"Those wretched Smurfs escaped me again!" he yelled, throwing himself on the floor in a tantrum. "I'll get you, you miserable Smurfs!"

Meanwhile the Smurfs celebrated their safe return to Smurf Village. Even the Wandering Smurf was happy.

"I'm so thankful to be home!" said the Wandering Smurf. "I'll never leave again!"